The Bridge

CW00867482

Meredith Hooper

Illustrated by Peter Kent

CAMBRIDGE
UNIVERSITY PRESS

A long time ago, the river Cam flowed through a wide and marshy valley. People crossed the river near a hill.

The river was narrow here, so it was a good place to cross.

Families built their houses on the hill, where the ground was dry. They grew crops and kept animals, and went hunting for birds and fish in the marshes.

3

The Romans came. They built a town
on the hill and a bridge over the river.

Boats carrying pottery, wine
and oil came along the river
all the way from the sea.
They tied up near the bridge.

4

The bridge fell down after the Romans left. A long time later, a new bridge was built across the river.

No-one knows exactly when the new bridge was built.

A busy town grew on both sides of the river.

6

Everyone used the bridge to get from
one side of the town to the other.

Boats unloaded cargoes of wool, hay
and corn at quays along the river bank.
There was a busy market on one side
of the river and a new castle on the hill.

7

The bridge often needed mending
because the wood rotted and broke.

8

The sheriff lived in the castle. He collected money from the townspeople to pay for mending the bridge but he kept this money for himself.

The bridge became so unsafe that everyone had to pay to cross the river in a ferry. The ferry was owned by the sheriff and he kept this money too.
  When the townspeople found out what the sheriff was doing they were very angry.

Hundreds of years later, a new bridge was built of stone because the wooden bridge kept rotting and breaking.

Barges could unload their cargoes at quays next to the new stone bridge. The barges were pulled along the river by horses. It was safe and cheap to carry heavy loads in barges and boats.

But the stone bridge was not strong enough.
So, this time iron was used to build a new bridge.

More and more wagons and carts with heavy loads were crossing the bridge.

More and more people were travelling in carriages and stage-coaches. The new bridge had to be strong enough to carry lots of traffic.

13

The iron bridge is still here. The bridge across the river Cam gave its name to Cambridge.

Index